THE BRIDE'S ORPHAN CHRISTMAS

MAIL ORDER BRIDES OF WYOMING

SUSANNAH CALLOWAY

Tica House Publishing

Sweet Romance that Delights and Enchants!

PERSONAL WORD FROM THE AUTHOR

Dearest Readers,

Thank you so much for choosing one of my books. I am proud to be a part of the team of writers at Tica House Publishing who work joyfully to bring you stories of hope, faith, courage, and love. Your kind words and loving readership are deeply appreciated.

I would like to personally invite you to sign up for updates and to become part of our **Exclusive Reader Club**—it's completely Free to join! We'd love to welcome you!

Much love,

Susannah Calloway

VISIT HERE to Join our Reader's Club and to Receive Tica House Updates:

https://wesrom.subscribemenow.com/

CHAPTER 1

Suddenly the room wasn't hot anymore, and William found himself listening to a familiar voice. *Too* familiar. He wasn't sitting anymore, either. He was lying on a soft straw bed, staring at the wood ceiling with a small niggling burn at the base of his abdomen. William knew where he was, but he couldn't stop the memories. He had to relive everything—his worst nightmare.

"Have you given him any painkillers?"

"No, Doc."

The invisible odor of antiseptic wafted from somewhere he couldn't see, reminding William he was in the crude hospital, bed-ridden and recently operated on. He saw the white coat of the friendly, overly genial doctor and shook his head.

If I had moved two seconds earlier, just two seconds, I'd be riding back to California with the rest of the men.

The letter—from the only mother figure he'd ever known—had told him not to blame himself, but who else was there to blame? It was easy for her to say. She was in Taos, New Mexico, with harmless little children, and he was here in Oregon, trying to gather his life together after a possibly crippling bullet wound.

"Ah."

William shook his head. He was sore and angry. Martha, the matron of the orphanage he called home, was only trying to cheer his spirit. He bit his lower lip and tried to find comfort by snuggling deeper into the bed. He didn't find it.

"Mr. Conway, you're awake."

The doctor was a balding man with a round face and slight stature. Someone with a stature so unimposing, he would never find himself in a situation like William's, because he'd never be chosen as a US Marshal. Maybe that was why he found William's case easy to smile about. William had a good mind to quip something less than polite just to match their moods, but Martha's upbringing at the orphanage didn't give him rein. He sucked up all the anger and nodded grimly.

"Yes, Doc. Although I've been a lot better."

"I understand, Mr. Conway. Everyone wishes this had not happened."

William seriously doubted that, with the smile at the edge of the man's lips. "Am I goin' home soon?"

The doctor flipped through the notes in his hand, reading things William knew were about him. The man was nervous. The news was bad.

"We've fished out the bullet, Mr. Conway, and sewn you up pretty neatly. There are no signs of infection, and you should be fine to leave in a couple of days."

"Will I be able to walk?"

The doctor chuckled and tapped William gently on his stiff shoulder. William winced but caught it just in time. The man was oblivious to his pain.

"You'll walk, run, anything you want to do. The injury will have no obvious effect on those muscular responses."

Living with Martha had taught William to read faces on lying children, to see the story behind the words. The doctor was stalling.

"You can tell me, Doc. I'm a grown man. I can take it."

Dr. Cotton sighed and looked at his notes again just in case he was reading wrong. William almost smiled at the man's visible unease. This man wouldn't last two weeks as a Marshal.

"The bullet hit your pubic area, Mr. Conway. Your, uh,

reproductive glands are, uh, destroyed, and you'll not be able to have your own children."

The news hit him like a blow and William felt himself spiraling, swirling in the room as he heard his name called from outside. It was ending. It always ended here.

"William, William?"

William raised his head off the chair rest, bringing his eyes to alertness and quickly taking in the appearance of the room. He saw the dark wooden reading table in front of him, the long bed at the room's corner, wide floor panels, slightly open window and fully open door. Brock Weasley was standing in front of him with a napkin across his shoulder and his vest wet around the neck from sweat. It was a hot afternoon and the raucous noise from below told William the tavern was full and still filling up. Something would only be off if Brock wasn't sweating. He had slept it off, not for the first time in Brock's tavern.

"He's around, downstairs. He's been waiting for some time."

"Send him up, Brock. Thank you."

Brock nodded and walked back to the door, pausing for a moment to speak before leaving.

"The others are around, William. You gonna do this quickly, won't ya? I don't want no trouble with the Haney gang."

William nodded. "I will," he added, when he realized a mere nod was not enough assurance for Brock. Brock owed William nothing and was doing him and the town a favor. William had no intention of getting him in any trouble.

Brock closed the door gently behind him, and William rubbed his hand across his face. He had that dream every day now. It was his past, but it clung to him like a bad smell. It determined his future, his *childless* future.

He stood up and walked to the window, making sure to keep in the shadows even though the window was barely open. No one had discovered that William met with one of the Haney gang members here in Brock's establishment. If they played it right, no one would. The informant would finally hand the Haney gang over to William and the town's watch, and Taos would be fine again.

The sound of feet tapping the wooden boards brought William back to alertness. He walked to a dark corner of the room and watched with his hand on his gun handle as the door opened. In came a young lad with long scrawny legs and a scratchy mess of brown hair. It was Marvis, his informant. William didn't move from where he was.

"What's the next hit, Marvis?"

Marvis didn't turn to look at William. There was no need. Both of them knew it would hardly take thirty seconds. It was safer that way.

"There's a train heading to Colorado, to pay some ol' miners there. We robbin' it. And we doin' it quick, too."

"Where are you gonna meet it?"

"It's passing through here so the plan is to stop the train, git as much money as we can git, and take off thousands of dollars richer."

William took a deep breath and tried to think. Such trains were common practice, but there were usually safe because they had guards. If the Haney gang were going for that train, it meant they were bringing a good number of guns.

"But a lot of people are on that train, and armed men. Passengers will be caught in the crossfire."

"Henry don't care. He says we go for the big catch once and for all. No more small game. And it's Christmas. He says we deserve a good Christmas gift. This is it."

William grunted and shifted his feet. This was bad, very bad. He had to alert the rest of the marshals and the sheriff.

"Can I leave now, Mr. Conway? I don't want no trouble."

"Go on."

The door shut almost immediately as the words left his lips. William waited for the sounds of his footsteps to die, then he walked to the bed and waited for a full hour, before slipping quietly out through the back and riding all the way home.

Martha would be waiting for him, worried for his safety, and fussing over him as she always did.

CHAPTER 2

The train sped quickly. It had gone past the brick chimney buildings and cobbled roads that Alice had seen all her life. Now it was running past a more rural area—farmlands, farm workers, shacks, and lots of white houses. Alice had heard this was what the Wild West looked like.

"Nothing but brown earth, cowboys and Indians... Who wants to go to the West anyway?"

Mary had said that. Alice had quickly shut up about leaving for Wyoming. There was nothing for her in New York anymore. Alice patted her bonnet and tried to remember what the pastor had told them in church last Sunday.

Something about the Lord's direction.

Alice remembered feeling like she needed the Lord's direction more than most. She didn't know what she was doing. Besides Quaker, whom she'd loved with her whole heart, her mother was the only family she had in the world. But her mother had been sickly for years, and Alice had lived in constant fear of the day when she'd finally have to bid her good-bye. Well, it had come last year, just before Christmas. Quaker had helped her survive through it.

Alice rubbed her hands together, remembering the feel of brown dirt between her fingers. She should have left in the morning, at least Fred's letter had told her to leave at dawn with the morning train. And she had replied that she would. But that morning, she'd been at Quaker's grave, weeping and finding no resolve to get going. When she finally did, she knew the train was gone but she went to the station anyway. She was lucky there was another train at noon. She was on it now.

Alice opened her purse and sought the brown paper that she had folded into a small square. She took it out and glanced through Fred's letter again, assuring herself that a new husband and a better Christmas awaited her in Sheridan, Wyoming.

November 9, 1867.

Dear Alice,

I can hardly wait for you arrival at Sheridan. Be assured I'll keep vigil at the train station till you get here. Do well to leave at dawn. The weather can get rather rough later in the day. Take care.

Love, Fred.

Mayor of Sheridan.

Alice dabbed her eyes. She had never stopped feeling deceitful while sharing correspondence with Fred. He had told her everything and all his letters were sunny and warm. She had only thought about Quaker when she wrote letters to him. And Fred was the mayor, that had to count for something. But it didn't, because Alice never cared how much a man had or how much power he wielded. Quaker had loved her, and she had loved him desperately. She had loved him till influenza had taken him away from her.

She had tried everything, herbs, pastes, roots, doctors. She had prayed like never before. It hadn't mattered. Her husband had withered before her eyes, going from a healthy handsome man to a weak, almost dry caricature. Like with her mother. She had known he was dying before he succumbed.

A young woman walked past her cubicle, carrying a tray of toffees but not bothering to look into the cubicle. Her dress reminded Alice of the docks and the life she had left behind.

Slowly, she had gathered herself after Quaker died and sought work. She had found a position as a saleswoman at the docks. It was there she had met Mary. But the life hadn't suited Alice, and she found herself growing weary of the insulting comments and lewd looks from the dock hands.

She told no one when she bought the first newspaper in search of Mail Order Bride adverts. No one knew when she replied to them, and no one knew when she started sharing missives with Fred. Alice told no one that she was leaving, and she felt no regret. There was no one to tell anyway. Mary wasn't truly her friend, and she was tired of New York. It only reminded her of her lost loved ones.

"Is anyone there, miss?"

Alice lifted her eyes to see another young woman. Blue eyes, dark brown locks, a brown cotton dress and a piece of luggage that must be very heavy for her, Alice wondered if this was how she looked, too.

"No, you can sit there. I do need some company."

"Thank you."

The young woman pulled her bag behind her and shifted into the seat opposite Alice. Alice tried to hide her staring as she wondered if this young woman was also a Mail Order Bride, but she knew she'd likely never know.

The lady looked tired and flushed. Alice wondered if she'd

had a long day or if she was tired of life in the East and was looking for a kinder Christmas in the wildness of the American West.

The noise of the children's chatter normally disturbed William, but tonight, he was grateful because it was keeping Martha busy. William cut through the loin of beef and slid it through the rich sauce when he heard a door close behind him. There wasn't any more noise and he knew Martha must have tucked all the orphans into bed. She was done for the day.

"How are ya today?"

William nodded and munched the sweet side of beef. That was a preliminary. They both knew what was coming next.

"I went to see the sheriff, but he wasn't in his office. I do hope he comes here. We've got something mighty serious to discuss," he said.

Martha's right brow rose, animating her wrinkled forehead.

"Trouble?"

William nodded and cut through another piece of beef. He took a sip of the cool milk before putting the meat in his mouth.

"Enough trouble for a lifetime. I've called for the rest of the marshals from Colorado. I hope they get here in time."

Martha worked her mouth, sending her lips twitching and William could see she was struggling to decide if she should inquire or not. She chose not to.

"Just be safe, William. Ya got a long life in front of you."

He knew he should let it slide, but he just couldn't hold it in. Her response was directed and tailored to get a response from him, and she was going to get it.

"A long life helping tend to the children here at the orphanage?" he asked.

"Don't speak of it like it's a bad thing. It ain't. And you know that."

William placed the plate to his side, in the middle of the bench. Martha sat at the other end. He had tried to rush as much as he could eat before Martha came and started this drill. He had lost his appetite now, and he hadn't eaten enough. He looked into the dark sky, many distant dots twinkling without fail. William loved the outdoors.

Maybe because it prevents me from coming in contact with the children here.

"You know I don't think this is a bad thing, Martha. But how do you expect me to git a wife when I cannot father a child. There is more to matrimony than living together and bedding your wife. Birthing and rearing a child is a good part of it."

Martha stretched and touched William on the shoulder, but William felt no comfort in it. Staying here at the orphanage was a pain for him because he was forced to see children every day. He never told Martha, but he was tormented every time he saw a child laugh or cry, or sing, or even when he saw them run into the fields and come back injured. Martha cooed over them like a mother hen, but he got more aloof by the day. He would never have his own child, and it was heart-breaking to be reminded every second of every day. Yet he couldn't leave. It would crush Martha, who was the only mother he had ever known.

"Just find a wife, William. I believe God will make a way."

William shrugged her hand off angrily and leapt to his feet. God would make a way? *God?* William saw Martha purse her lips together, readying herself for whatever he had to say. And he had a lot of words. He opened his mouth to speak when he heard the pounding hooves of a horse coming from the entrance of the place. Martha took his plate and stood while William turned and clutched his gun. The rider slowed as he got to them, and William saw it was the sheriff.

"William."

"Sheriff Nate, I'd been expecting you long before now."

The door shut behind him. Martha had gone in. William felt great relief. They would have their argument another day.

"I had a busy day, William."

The sheriff got off his horse and tied his steed to the stairwell post. He took off his hat and stared frankly into William's eyes.

"How bad is it?"

"Haney bad. I called for the rest of the marshals yesterday. They should get to Taos at dawn tomorrow morning, just in time to meet up with us and a few willing town hands. The Haney gang is planning to stop and rob a train moving with money for a coupla' miners in Colorado. It's to happen at our border. Let's make sure it happens within New Mexico. This is our chance to get these varmints."

Sheriff Nate nodded and pulled a spoke from a blade of grass. He slid it between his lips and stood with his arms loose.

"Marshals and a train with money? William, there's going to be a lot of shooting."

"Not if we can sneak up on them."

Sheriff Nate chuckled. William could tell what he was wondering. How does a posse of a hundred something men sneak up on a train?

"Or if we can get close enough," William added, trying to salvage hope.

The sheriff sighed and placed his hat back on his head. He started for his horse and William came after him.

"It doesn't matter how dire it looks, Willy. We can't allow Haney to run rampant on our land. It's five weeks to Christmas. We have to do this."

William waited till the sheriff mounted his horse before replying.

"I've informed the marshals to go straight to your office. I'll be there before them tomorrow morning. We move for the railroads once everyone is gathered."

Light shot out from the orphanage house, maybe one of the children playing somewhere. It ran across the sheriff's face and William saw that he wasn't alone in his dread. Even the sheriff looked deeply concerned.

"Go and find sleep, William. Tomorrow is a serious day."

William watched as the sheriff's horse galloped along the dusty path till he saw and heard it no more. He turned to go in.

Henry Haney was an angry man. That was his defining feature, the essence of his living and what made him tick. He knew it and embraced it. Henry steadied the horse beneath him and watched as his men gathered sleepily. It annoyed him, got him vexed, just how he liked to be.

"What is the lot of ya doing? Git this buffoonery to a head and let's go. We've got money to make."

He could have used 'steal' instead of 'make' but it didn't matter. Stealing money was making money. Henry saw that the rest of his twenty-four men were ready to go before rearing up his horse.

"Heeyah!" he screamed and set the horse off in a furious gallop. The rest of his men came after him in a brown dusty cloud.

They had slept in the mountains, managing to find comfort in the warmth their numbers provided. This was best, as it provided them the closest access to the point where they planned to stop the train. There were so many things that were wrong about this plan, but Henry didn't mind. His entire life had been one big risk.

Fred Harrington had told them about this train and wanted them to rob it as they did all the establishments and trains he told them about. Rob it, share the gains in half. Fred Harrington was the mayor of Sheridan, Wyoming, but he was as slimy as Henry. He knew he would lose his reelection bid, so he planned to use the money to bribe his way into reelection next year. But Henry didn't care, the Haney gang was tired of sharing.

Why would I share when I can take all of it, less whatever I deem fit to give my men?

After a week of pretended contemplation and extended fact finding, Henry informed Mayor Harrington that the Haney gang viewed the venture as too dangerous. They weren't doing it. Fred was vexed and threatened Henry; Henry threatened back. Now, Henry and his men were going for the exact same train, only this time, they weren't in a deal with the mayor.

"He'd know, for sho," one of his men had said.

Henry didn't care. The mayor might know, but he couldn't do anything about it. If Fred came for them, Henry would make sure both parties went down.

"That's the track," someone shouted, causing Henry to lift his eyes.

Henry saw it. Yes, the track, their path to a life of riches. Henry raised his hand, signaling his men to slow down as they approached. He slowed down to a trot and led his horse behind a stack of rocks. His men also got lost behind the geography.

They didn't have to wait.

"We're right on time," Henry whispered to himself when he saw the chute of smoke at the horizon. Henry turned and saw his men wearing excited grins. They were going to be rich.

They waited for the train to get about one fourth of a mile to where they were, before galloping toward the track. They had placed a huge boulder on a wooden ramp the day before and quickly attached three horses to the other end of the ramp. The horses ran forward, causing the spherical rock to roll into the track. Then they took out their guns, stood beside the track and waited.

CHAPTER 3

The sudden stop caused Alice's head to snap back and hit the back of her seat. "Ouch!"

Alice rubbed at her head and tried to get her bearings when she heard the first gun shot, then a whole lot of gun shots.

"Everyone, ya all do well to stick to yo seats. We only want the money."

What money?

The young woman across the table from Alice was pale white. Alice looked out of the window and saw a man with a shiny shotgun grinning at her. She dropped low, covered her beating heart with her palm, and struggled to breathe calmly. There was a ruckus from the next cubicle, a scream, someone grunting, two loud bangs, and a much louder scream.

"Keep yo mouth shut. Dean, come shut this gal up."

This was a robbery. Alice didn't have anything, but the men wouldn't believe her. She wasn't going to wait for Dean to come for her, too. She started to crawl out of the cubicle. She could still hear Dean in the next cubicle, but Alice didn't stop. She crawled past many cubicles full of frozen, terrified passengers, and finally found herself at the door of another coach. Not knowing what lay behind the door, but guessing she'd fare better there, Alice opened the door and fell inside. The car was filled with bags of coal, unused coal. Alice found respite, no one would search for her here.

"Henry, a posse of men is on its way."

Alice almost cried. The men must have been just behind the other door. Why did she come here?

"It's the sheriff and his boys. We knew they was coming, but we decided to risk it and we're still risking it."

"They're close, Henry. Do you think Fred did this?"

"Fred Harrington is a part of us. He might have informed us about the loot and gotten slighted in the process. But he for sho ain't going to tell the sheriff. Get as much money as you can get. Let 'em come. We have hostages."

Fred Harrington? How many Fred Harringtons could there possibly be?

Alice closed her eyes and wished she had never come on this trip. She wished her mother had not died, and Quaker had never left her alone. She wished she had listened to Mary and remained a lifeless saleswoman on the docks. Alice was still closing her eyes when shots rang out again.

She lay flat on the sooty floor and tried not to sneeze as men yelled and the noise of galloping engulfed the coach.

"Don't come any closer. For every yard ya move, we gonna kill five men."

Alice tried to rest when the noise settled down after the declaration, but it was only a few minutes before a bullet rang out again. Suddenly, the commotion was in the train, and she felt the vibration of many feet moving. Horses started to run again, and she heard the vivid whiz of a bullet lodging itself in a man just beside the coach wall. She heard him fall, sliding along the wall of the coach. Alice started to weep. This was a nightmare.

The shooting and commotion continued for what seemed to be forever. Alice wept more when a bullet blasted through the window of her coach, shattering the glass and spraying it all over her. There was a grunt behind the door where she'd come in. Then there was a crash on the door; men were fighting.

The door shook on its hinges then suddenly there was a knife blade sticking out of the door and into her coach. The blade was slick with blood and then withdrawn. There was a dull slump and one man shouting loudly. Alice covered her mouth and cried silently. She closed her eyes and finally darkness swallowed her.

When Alice opened her eyes, there was utter silence, and the coach was half dark. She sat up and tried to imagine all that had happened. Her mind failed miserably in trying to think of what next to do. She let out her grief with deep sniffs and sobs.

"Hello?"

What? Was there someone around?

Alice didn't know whether to keep quiet or to call for help. What if it was one of the robbers? Alice kept mum and stayed still.

"Is someone there? I heard a small sound now."

It was a male voice and rather kind, but Alice was too startled to respond. She stayed still and watched wide-eyed as the door facing her opened and a tall man with a wide brimmed hat squinted at her. The man's eyes ran across her body, looking particularly interested in her face. Alice imagined that her face would be streaked with black soot, dust, and smeared with tears. The man was probably shocked at her appearance.

"Howdy there. Are you hurt?"

Alice eyed the gun safely tucked in the man's holster. He stretched his hand and maintained a kind smile. Finally deciding he was safe, Alice reached out and took his hand, allowing him to lead her out.

Outside of the coach, there were many men and women. Alice noticed men with guns helping people out of the train. There were carriages, where a few injured people were being placed. This was a safe company.

"What's your name, ma'am?"

"Alice. Alice Thompson, sir."

The man nodded and appeared to study her. Alice wilted under his gaze. She had never felt so filthy. Unable to meet his eye, she looked across the land and watched as two carriages full of people sporting injuries slowly went away in the same direction.

"How are you, Miss Thompson? Are you injured?"

Alice shook her head and the deep pain of a headache caused her knees to buckle. She whimpered and almost fell to the ground only to be caught by the man.

"I'm Mr. William Conway. Do you need to go to see the doc?"

Alice tried to respond, but she hardly heard the mumblings of her mouth. She saw his mouth move as the light faded and her eye lids grew heavier. The only word she made out was "Home."

Alice didn't know where home was anymore.

CHAPTER 4

William's breath catch as she stirred. This was the first time she had moved since he brought her home the evening before. He wouldn't have brought her if he had known she had a head injury, but it wasn't too late. Martha insisted the injury wasn't beyond her experience with bruises and cuts and other injuries of the children.

"Pretty little thing, she for sho doesn't like being scared to her wits yesterday," came Martha's voice.

Martha walked across to the bed and sat on the squat stool beside Alice's head. And right on cue, Alice opened her eyes.

"Praise God, she's awake."

William drew closer and watched Alice's eyelids flutter at Martha. Then slowly, she turned her head to stare at him.

Realization struck William with unexpected force. She was beautiful, astonishingly pretty. Even with her scared, wide-eyed stare, her sky-blue eyes animated the flawless milky white tone of her skin. Her face had a slender round shape with ears, eyes and lips only adding to her allure. The long curls of strawberry blonde hair that spilled around her ears and barely reached her shoulders felt like the finishing of an artwork. He had not noticed this yesterday when he had been so concerned about her health, and she had been almost completely covered in soot.

She gazed at him and opened her mouth as if to say something then suddenly jumped up off the bed and covered her mouth with her palm. She shot out of the door with William and Martha racing after her.

"Did you say something to her?" William hollered after Martha.

Martha had almost caught up with Alice when she finally replied no. But then, they were already outside and were watching Alice retch all over the soil just beside the porch. She was not running away. She had wanted to go vomit. William looked back to see the children standing on the porch, staring at Alice as another wave of vomiting started.

"Damian, go git me a bowl of water. Sandy, please bring a clean rag."

A lanky sandy-haired boy ran in first and his seven-year-old sister ran into the house after him. William walked to

Alice and leaned beside her after she was done. He placed his hand on her back and tapped her as if to say, "Let it all out."

The boy and his sister were back with the bowl and rags. William straightened up and allowed Martha to rinse Alice's face and mouth. Then she mopped her skin with the rag.

"You can look up now, Miss Thompson. Everyone here is a friend."

Alice raised her eyes and smiled timidly at Martha and William.

"I'm sorry. I'm very sorry."

"No, no, there ain't any reason to be sorry. You sure are sick, and we're gonna see the doctor. But first, we'll have you cleaned up and your belly full."

William smiled, and Alice looked somewhat lost. This was Martha's territory, and she made sure everyone had a full belly. Alice looked at William and stuttered at first, but then she let out the words.

"Thank you, f-for yesterday. I can't seem to remember anything after you saved me."

William nodded. He started to speak then was aware of the audience so he looked at the children.

"Go on in, children. Lacy, get all of them in."

Lacy was the eldest. She was a mature fourteen-year-old who was taking after Martha in many ways.

"Let's go in, children. We could go read some books."

There were a few grumbles, but soon the porch was empty, and the door shut. William cast his eyes back on Alice.

"I brought you home yesterday because I didn't know you were injured. It was" – he looked at Martha – "Martha, who noticed the bump and cut on the back of your head. But by then, you were asleep. We decided we could treat it, or leave it till morning when you woke up yourself. But now, you're vomiting. You have to see the doctor."

"For sho. Eat, then see the doctor."

One hour later, they were being ushered into the reception at the clinic. There was a line, and they had to wait. William decided to make a quick trip. He could easily be back before Alice were done. He walked through the room to where Alice was seated with Martha standing beside her.

"I need to go see the sheriff. I'll take the buckboard, but I'll be mighty quick."

"We are fifth in line," Martha said.

"I know."

William looked down at Alice who looked away immediately when his eyes met hers. He nodded and walked out of the room, very conscious of her eyes on his receding figure. He walked out of the long structure that served as Taos' only hospital and got into the wagon. He flapped the reins on the horse, and it moved, pulling the wagon along.

What was he to make of Miss Thompson? She didn't look shy, but she wasn't bold per se. And her eyes caught everything. He hadn't bothered to ask why she was on the train because he had been sure she'd only stay that night. But now, Martha was acting very protectively, and he wouldn't pretend to be in a rush to have her out anyway. It was pleasant having someone to talk to aside from Martha, if she would actually talk to him.

He almost missed a turn and quickly directed the horse in the right way. The tall oak tree with a stubborn burnt branch told him he was at the sheriff's place. William secured the horse and jumped down.

"I'll be right back," he said, running his fingers over the stallion's nose, before bounding up the steps and knocking on the old wooden door.

"Come on in."

William pushed the door open and as always, the scent of cookies welcomed him. The room was empty except for Sheriff Nate, who was leaning back into his rocking chair, cross-legged on his table. He looked much too comfortable for William's liking.

"For you to be sitting here, looking restful and eating cookies, the news had better be good."

"I'm always eating cookies and looking restful. And I've not got much of good news lately."

William took a seat and picked up a cookie. He bit into it. It was delicious. Sheriff Nate's wife had perfected baking cookies to an art.

"Did we get any of them?"

"If ya mean, did we git any of them in the crossfire? Yes. Patrick Louvre is dead. He was a confirmed member of the gang. We have two other bodies yet to be identified. But all the rest got away. They went through the mountains, across a brook and a rocky outcrop."

William shook his head.

"They had this all planned. Your insider gave you the right news but not soon enough. And don't bother asking about the money. They took all of it. Those Colorado miners are going to have one sorry Christmas."

William bit into the cookie. It didn't taste so good now.

"Congratulations, Miss Thompson, you're with child. It's a shame your husband had to go off for his business. I do love telling couples together."

Alice saw that the shocked look on Martha's face matched how she felt. She crumpled into the seat and didn't bother explaining to the doctor that William wasn't her husband. She had only met him yesterday. Alice shook her head. Things just couldn't get worse.

"All right. Thank ya, doctor," Martha said, half pulling Alice out of the chair and getting her out of the room. The last person went in after they came out and they were left alone in the outer cubicle. Alice looked up and tears dripped down both cheeks.

"No, no, stop crying, child."

"You don't understand. My, my, my husband, late husband – he's dead. This was ..."

She sniffed again and Martha pulled her into her embrace, allowing her tears to dampen the front of her cotton dress.

"Don't worry. Ya can stay at the orphanage for as long as ya want. I can see this is a surprise to you. Even if you don't know, God knows."

Alice cried more and was soon trembling. Martha did nothing but hug her and console her.

Alice was distraught. What she heard about Fred Harrington yesterday, confirmed that he was in league with the robbers. It had to be the same Fred Harrington she was supposed to marry. There was no way she was going to marry a thief.

Because of that, she had planned to go back to New York; maybe to start another life.

But now she was with child, and she couldn't possibly return. Nor could she go on to Wyoming because her proposed husband was a dangerous villain. She could only stay. But William—he was obviously a lawman; a marshal would be her guess. She was surprised he hadn't asked any questions. If he found out she was pregnant, he would ask questions. Alice was desperate to keep her secrets.

"Please, Martha, please promise not to tell William about my pregnancy."

"Why? William should know—"

"Please, Martha, I beg of you."

Hard footsteps made Martha look up. She quickly rubbed her face with her sleeves and averted her eyes. William got to them and spoke.

"So what did the doctor say?"

"He says she just needs rest. She'll be fine. She can stay at the orphanage for some time till she sorts out some things."

Alice smiled and thanked the dear Lord for Martha.

CHAPTER 5

"Ya eat too much for a nine-year-old, Damian."

Alice smiled as Damian stood beside Martha with eyes so hungry, one could bet he hadn't had anything that day. Yet he'd just had the biggest dinner in the house.

"Come on here, Damian."

"Don't make that boy a glutton, William. He better learn to be content like the Bible teaches him."

William shook his head and shoveled a good chunk of his porridge onto Damian's plate.

"Thank you, Mr. Conway."

William nodded. Martha scowled and the boy ran off to the

kitchen where he'd likely wolf down the porridge. Alice laughed out loud, drawing looks from William and Martha.

"It ain't funny. That boy will eat up our farm."

"Then we'll plant another garden," William said.

Martha cast a warning glance at William that told him he was on a short leash. Wisely, he kept mute. Alice shook her head and spooned a bite of her porridge into her mouth. It hadn't taken her long to discover the way things were. William was like an elder brother to all the children in the orphanage and a lenient one.

He didn't act like it, but he was wonderful with children and they all loved him. Alice had caught herself pondering if he would be so wonderful with her unborn child. She'd done it so many times, it didn't alarm her anymore. Alice also found herself taking longer glances at him. She liked him, that much she couldn't deny.

She had caught him staring at her many times, too. And he was confident enough not to look away when their eyes met. He was handsome and thoughtful. His mouth only seemed to say little of what his head thought and that added to the intrigue Alice found in him. He still hadn't asked her about her former life. After two weeks, Alice was starting to feel safe that he never would. She didn't know why she was so hesitant to share her former life. Perhaps, she wanted to keep it inside, near her heart, where no one could touch it.

"Come on, Alice. Christmas isn't waiting for us. And the children sure won't forgive us if we don't finish."

Alice quickly stuck the last spoonful of porridge into her mouth and rushed to the kitchen. She dropped her dish into a bowl of sudsy water and turned to see William coming in behind her. He was staring so hard at the cup in his hand, it was obvious he was trying not to look at her.

"You need to get water?"

"Don't bother yourself, Miss Thompson. I'll get it myself."

Alice watched him walk to the barrel and fetch some water for himself. He turned back and sipped from it. Their eyes met as he drank, and he smiled.

"Is something on my face?" he asked.

Alice shook her head. She opened her mouth to speak but his eyes on her made her tongue freeze. She took a deep breath and tried again.

"You can call me Alice. Please, call me Alice."

He stopped sipping. The light caught on the line of wetness that hung on his mustache. Alice swallowed hard. The man got to her.

"All right, Alice. I'm William. Oh, you know I'm William. But call me William."

She nodded and grinned.

"You've got a little... Something is on your lip, Alice."

Alice ran the back of her hand over her lips and looked at him again. He nodded and tapped the right side of his upper lip. She wiped again, and he shook his head. He didn't try to show her again. He took a step to her and was too many inches closer. Alice could feel the warmth from his big frame.

"Can I ... can I get it off?"

She nodded. The air stilled as his finger ran across the top of mouth. Her skin froze as his calloused fingers ran the length of her upper lip. When he brought the finger back to show her the small bit of porridge, she was staring into his smiling brown eyes. He had numerous tiny crinkles at the sides of his eyes that she was seeing as if for the first time.

"Alice! We've not got all day."

Martha's shout from the sitting room startled Alice, and she quickly remembered she was meant to be with Martha as they had been every evening for the past four days. Bags, socks, mitts, and scarves were waiting to be knitted. Martha did the harder job of making corn husk dolls for the younger girls and embroidering hankies.

"I do have to go."

"I'll be right after you."

Alice slipped out of the kitchen and took a deep breath. William normally sat across them working on the carved wooden toys he made every year for the kids while the women knitted and talked. How could Alice possibly concentrate on her knitting when he did so this evening?

William whittled the toy soldier's neck a bit too deep.

"Arrggh." He groaned and felt their eyes fall on him. He looked up. Martha was getting to her feet while Alice was focusing on her knitting, focusing a bit too hard in his opinion. He had been overly aware of Alice's presence since their brief talk in the kitchen. That was the longest discussion he had shared with her during the two weeks she had been there, and he now wondered why. He'd always wanted to ask her when she was leaving, but now her leaving was the last thing he wanted.

"William, would ya mind sitting over here with Alice? I need to make plum pudding and I much prefer that bench."

William gathered the remaining short sticks and tools he planned to work with that evening and walked across the room to settle down beside Alice. It wasn't until he was sitting that it struck him that he might have gotten up a bit too eagerly. Martha walked out of the room to fetch something, and he was left with Alice.

The silence was awkward, and William found his nerves getting frayed by the second. He stole a glance at Alice and saw she was just staring at her fingers. She wasn't knitting.

"Uh, thank you for offering to help Martha with making the gifts. It's normally very hard work for her."

Alice looked up at him and gave him the bright smile he'd come to expect but was always unprepared for.

"Oh, it's one of the ways I can say thank you to both of you."

"Why?"

"You let me stay here, William, without any knowledge of me. Not really."

William wanted to tell her that old things were passed away, just like the Bible said, but he decided he had a more personal answer.

"I had no choice but to agree. Martha has the biggest heart in the West. I'm as much a stranger here as you."

"Stranger? You've lived here all your life."

William cut out the shoulder of the marching man, doing it quite expertly despite the lack of concentration he cast on it.

"I was a stranger here even though I've lived here all my life."

He looked at Alice, and her eyes were curious. She shook her head and blinked. "I don't understand, William."

"I was the first child in this orphanage, Alice. But don't tell Martha that, she'd never agree. I'm her son, and that's all she'll hear of it."

Alice chuckled. "Yes, I can see that," she added.

"My parents were devout Christians at the church. My mother was Martha's best friend. When my parents died in a rock fall, Martha took me as hers. That was twenty-four years ago. Martha is my mother, and it started from that day. And you've spent how many days here?"

Alice laughed and bumped her shoulder against William. William could see that the story had surprised her, but she had assimilated it and now it had borne a tumble of thoughts he could see dancing in her blue eyes. One of which he hoped wasn't leaving soon.

"So, can you do the same William? Be a parent to a stranger?"

William looked back at his wooden soldier and tried to think of how many more he had to make. Alice's question struck him a little too close to home, and he wasn't prepared to handle it. He said nothing and shaved the wooden toy.

"Can you, William?" she pushed.

He turned to look at her. Her eyes glistened but probably it was his eyes glistening and appearing to be hers. William didn't trust his control at the moment. He took a deep breath and looked back at the soldier.

"I've got no choice, have I? I live in an orphanage."

His response brought a smile to her face but ripped open an injury in his heart that felt mighty raw.

CHAPTER 6

I was a fool to trust Henry. He's always been as slimy as they come.

Fred Harrington held *The Western Times* in front of him where the front page was splashed with news of the infamous train raid that the Haney gang had just successfully pulled off. He bit his lip and slapped his head again. *Why did I inform Henry about the train?* But he knew why he'd done it. He had done it many times.

He used his position as mayor to come to knowledge about the placement of huge amounts of money or valuables. Then he surreptitiously passed that knowledge to Henry who'd raid the place and bring half of the recovered loot to him. Sometimes it was less than half, but who was counting, definitely not Fred. They'd done it so many times, he'd gotten comfortable with Henry.

I got comfortable with the most deceitful of them all.

When Henry had informed him the Haney gang was not interested in the train, he had been caught off guard. The Haney gang had not seen a deposit of money they weren't interested in. Now, he had been double-crossed and the funds he needed to bribe the necessary people were missing. His re-election bid was running off track because he definitely wasn't going to win democratically. He was Mayor of Sheridan but no one in Sheridan liked it. Fred didn't mind as long as he remained mayor; they could hold back their affection.

He flapped the paper again, and his office door swung open. Fred frowned, but he knew who it was. Only two people came into his office without knocking, the double-crossing failed business partner and his favorite bounty hunter, Clarence Griffin.

Clarence took off his hat, balanced the crossbow beside his table and flopped into the chair in front of him.

"Hey, Clarence," Fred said briskly, pushing a small picture across the table toward him. Clarence picked it up. They'd done this dance many times. Everything was rehearsed now.

"Where's she? How much?" Clarence said.

Those were always the two questions Clarence asked. Normally, Fred just gave him that information and Clarence went and kidnapped, threatened or, on the rare occasion, got rid of the person for him. But now, Fred saw the need to provide more information.

"She's going to be my bride, a Mail Order Bride, Clarence. Her name is Alice Thompson, and she was on her way here from New York. I suspect she was on the train the Haney gang attacked. So, she's in between here and New Mexico, mostly likely that town the injured were taken to in New Mexico. What's the name again?"

"Taos."

"Yes, Taos," Fred said with such bitterness that Clarence's eyebrows rose.

"I need her to help with my re-election bid. People need to believe I'm a family man."

"You're not a family man, Fred. You're a criminal."

Fred sucked it in and took it as one of the hazards of their unholy fellowship.

"Your opinion matters not, especially not to the Sheridan ballot boxes come the new year. Just go there and get me my girl."

"How did you get this picture?"

I stole it, Fred wanted to say. "She sent it to me during our correspondence." It seemed surprisingly funny to Clarence.

"You wrote love letters?" Clarence asked, sniggering.

"Of course, I didn't. Someone wrote them for me. I hardly even read them. I'm too busy for such matters."

"Yeah, you are. You're too busy hiring me to kidnap people on your behalf."

Fred had a good mind to throw Clarence out of his office, but that would be stupid. He needed Clarence more than Clarence needed him.

"I'll pay you double your fee, Clarence. And a mighty big top up if I go on to win my re-election bid."

Clarence licked his lips and jumped to his feet. "You should have said that long ago. I wouldn't have sat here asking you needless questions."

Fred watched as Clarence put the picture of the girl in his coat pocket, picked up his weapon and swaggered out of his room.

"Aren't you going to go in? The sun's on its way out."

Alice shook her head, feeling her golden locks rub her neck and cover her ears. William sat on his stallion, dressed to go but he'd been waiting in front of the porch for many minutes now. Talking to her was more important than whatever he planned to go do that day.

"I want to feel the sun. It's something I always wish I did more."

Alice saw a question swim to the surface, saw it rise in his throat and form in his mouth. But then he swallowed it with a smile and pressed down his hat.

"Maybe, when I'm back, we can go into the fields together and feel the sun."

Alice's heart flipped many times. She blushed, looked to her feet and noticed her slowly swelling belly. She could hide it now, especially since she was lucky not to suffer morning sickness like many women did. But she was honest with herself. She only had about a month more to hide it from William.

Why was she hiding it from him? Was it just because she was scared he'd ask questions about her past? Questions that might lead her to talk about her trip here to be the bride of Fred Harrington. The very Mayor of Sheridan who turned informant for the thieving and blood-crazed Haney gang. Alice shuddered. She'd gone over the scenario many times. It never ended well.

She liked William. She liked the way he smiled when he looked at her, the way her heart tripped over his words, the way he was starting to touch her more and more. He'd held her hand for many minutes last night. Would he do that if he discovered she was carrying another man's child and was betrothed to someone else? No, she was of no use to him.

When Alice raised her eyes, she wasn't smiling anymore.

"Yes, we can," she said.

William blinked at her, nodded, and took off. Just as Alice saw his horse rush out between the gate poles, a wave of rare nausea throttled up her throat. She ran down the stairs and lowered her head to a barren patch. She didn't retch much, just saliva and a bit of the milk she had taken that morning. Milk that William had decided to get from the cow for her, just for her. Alice spat again and took a deep breath.

"What am I doing?" she asked in confused self-reflection.

"You'll be fine."

Martha came up behind her and handed her a small bowl of water. Alice hadn't even heard her come out of the house. She tried to smile, but it felt more like a grimace as she took the bowl from her. She rinsed her face and mouth then stood back upright. She suddenly felt at the edge of tears.

"What am I doing, Martha? I'm confused. Maybe I should tell him, maybe I shouldn't. And—" Her voice cracked and the images in her eyes started to swim.

"Oh, my dear. You'll be fine. God has a plan." Martha hugged her and Alice cried on her shoulder. She felt even worse now. She had told no one about her discovery in the train, not even Martha who was meant to be her confidante. She was scared what they'd do if they found she came to the west to be a Mail Order Bride for a man as unscrupulous as Fred Harrington.

"Are you sure, Martha? Because I'm not. I'm confused, and I'm sorry."

"Don't be sorry, dear. God has a plan for sho, for sho."

Martha rubbed her palm into the small of Alice's back, and the panic started to ebb.

CHAPTER 7

"She's still at the orphanage?"

William nodded and threw the apple high before catching it with one hand. Sheriff Nate's eyes followed the fruit, and William winked at him when their eyes met again. The sheriff couldn't do it. His hands were not steady enough.

"You still can't shoot half as well as I can."

"I could, until I got shot."

It was a lie. The bullet injury had done nothing to affect William's aim. But the sheriff wasn't to know that.

"To be frank, I don't want her to leave."

The sheriff grunted and toggled his brows rapidly at William. He bit into his apple, cutting out almost half.

"Why would you? You be looking for a bride. Why not a well-bred damsel from the east coast?"

William laughed. He liked the sound of that. He liked Alice, liked her enough to marry her, but he had his own problems and he wasn't going to force her into a life without her own children. He just couldn't.

"Don't be getting ideas, Nate. She's only been with us for four weeks."

"That's longer than I'd known my wife by the time I asked her to marry me. Now we've got four kicking boys, and we're not even done."

They both guffawed. William shook his head at the sheriff's silliness but noticed the smile wander off the sheriff's face as his eyes focused on a spot above William's head. William turned to see a man with a crossbow and a stalk of wheat between his lips standing behind him.

"Who's been with you for four weeks? Maybe it's my girl."

William frowned and turned back to see Sheriff Nate get to his feet. The sheriff was a very homely person and rarely frowned unless he truly needed to. He wasn't happy to see this man, and he wasn't hiding it.

The man still had the grin-smirk on his face. He looked like he had once been handsome but with skin sun-beaten till it was a copper brown and hardened by exposure to the cold of the plains, he had the appearance of a brute. His eyes were sleepy, heavy-lidded but unsettled, running across the entire room without missing one spot.

The crossbow in his right hand had about a dozen arrows in the pocket above, and William didn't doubt that he could use it. His eyes never concentrated on William once, well they never concentrated on anything for long, but William wasn't under any assumptions that the man couldn't pick him out in a crowd. He had that feel about him.

Bounty hunter.

The more William thought about it, the surer he became. The man walked, a triple step march that was almost a dance. He slid noiselessly into the chair beside William before turning to look at William and stretching his hand.

"Good morning, sir."

"I didn't ask you to sit, Clarence," Sheriff Nate said. His tone was icy.

"That's why I took the seat, Sheriff. Come on. I'm not here to cause any trouble. I'm here for business, that's all."

"Your business is trouble, Clarence."

Clarence laughed and smiled. "No trouble this time, I promise."

"If I found a sliver of gold for every time you made that promise, Clarence, I'd own the West."

William wanted to laugh, but it seemed inappropriate. Sheriff Nate gave Clarence a long gaze, looked at William as if to say, "I tried," then fell back into his seat.

"What brings you here, Clarence? Why are you in Taos anyway? Last I heard, a bounty had you rampaging in Sheridan."

Clarence offered a satisfied grin. He enjoyed his work, that much was clear. He fished a small card out of his pocket and slid it across the table to the sheriff. Nate picked it up, interest flickered in his eyes, but control returned the next instant. He slid the picture halfway back and interlocked his fingers over his chest.

"The new bounty?"

"You're a smart sheriff. I came to give you information and maybe, get information. If you've seen my woman around, I'd be mighty glad if you could, ya know, send me her way."

Sheriff Nate scoffed. "I'm the sheriff, Clarence. And if I catch you in the act of collecting folks without the sanction of the law, I'm obligated and empowered by the law to git you arrested. I'm most definitely not sending anyone your way. And I'd advise you to do everything by the book, despite how unlikely that is."

The sheriff placed a hand over the picture and slid it the rest of the way, but toward William instead of Clarence. It was strange, and William stretched to take it.

"Don't come picking up people from our town for your less-than-holy reasons, Clarence."

William took the picture and stared at it. Alice's eyes blazed back at him. William coughed and almost scrunched up the picture in his fist. He dropped it back on the table and looked at Clarence. The man had his brows almost touching. William knew he should have been more composed, but how could a man discover that the prize of a bounty hunter was in his house and remain composed.

"Is she familiar, sir?"

William shook his head and almost flung the picture back at the hunter.

"No, I've not seen her before. Have you, Nate?"

"No, never, but not that I would tell Clarence if I had," Sheriff Nate replied. The comment drew a smile from the bounty hunter.

"This isn't an illegal search, Sheriff. This woman is the betrothed bride of Mr. Fred Harrington, the Mayor of Sheridan. Last he knew, she got on a train on the way to Sheridan, Wyoming. But there's a high probability she got waylaid during the recent heist by the Haney gang."

That's exactly what happened, William thought.

"The mayor asked me to go look for his bride and bring her

to him. It's nothing illegal. We just want to get a willing bride to her husband."

She wasn't so willing to William's knowledge. He saw no reason why Alice had never mentioned this to him or Martha, except there was something the bounty hunter wasn't telling. And there usually was. The bounty hunter took the picture and slipped it back into his coat.

"I'm going to be on my way now, Sheriff," He tipped his hat to William. "But if you come in contact with her anywhere, please send me a message. I'll be in town, at the Silent Inn."

He did his marching walk and the door slammed behind him. They both waited for a few moments until they heard his horse neigh as he rode away from the office. Then the sheriff was the first to speak.

"Someone has got a lot of explaining to do."

"Not me, Sheriff. She's got a lot of explaining to do to me. Please say nothing about her to this man."

"You should trust that I won't. His words could all be lies for all I know of him."

William shook his head and gave a shaky smile. He doubted it. What the bounty hunter said was the truth, at least most of it, he was sure.

CHAPTER 8

"Are you sure you can do this? Ya sho don't look like a farm girl."

Alice laughed. She wasn't, and she wasn't going to pretend to be. But she was here now, and she was ready to learn. She didn't know how much longer she'd stay here, but she intended to help anyway she could on the farm and in the house. Although, she still didn't know the best way to control the children. Some of them never listened. The cool-headed ones like Lacy and Damian needed no supervision, and the others didn't listen to her, only when they felt like it. They listened to Lacy a lot more, and Alice still didn't understand why. But Martha told her not to worry.

"Children make up their own minds. Give them time."

So Alice decided she'd just be friends with them and as

Martha said, with time, they'd learn to respect her authority. She preferred to put her energy into things that couldn't refuse it, things like woven clothes and corn dolls, or cows to be milked in this case.

"You just need to teach me, that's all. That way you can focus on making those dolls. You said Mary asked for two."

"She did and she's being a very good girl. I want to give her two, but Christmas is fast approaching and there's almost no more time," Martha said.

Alice nodded, glad Martha's words were strengthening her position.

"Then when we're done finishing last night's mitts, you could show me how to milk the two cows. I'll milk them and you can go on to work on the dolls."

"Are you sure, Alice? Ya don't really need to do this."

Alice smiled widely and pulled Martha's arm. "I want to do it. Please let me do this."

Martha snorted and started off in the direction of the shed at the back. Alice went after her, safe in the knowledge that Martha had tacitly given consent to her request. About an hour later, they were both knitting rapidly as their conversation wandered from one topic to another. When Martha sighed before speaking, Alice knew she was about to say something serious.

"So, how's our baby?"

Our baby?

Alice felt Martha's time-wizened eyes peering at her. She raised her eyes to her and saw the kindness that always encouraged her to open up. Martha was a bit bigger than her mother, but they had the same soft, encouraging stare that made you feel safe. In a way, Martha had become her mother.

"Our baby's fine. I don't feel too much discomfort lately."

"You're lucky. William would have found out if the baby is as turbulent as typical first pregnancies are."

Alice nodded. Keeping this secret wasn't something she was happy about. She was growing closer to William every day, and she had been lucky that her nausea that morning occurred just after he had left. How long could she hope to hide it from him? Nothing was built on lies. Quaker always used to say that.

Quaker. When last did I think of you, Quaker?

Alice didn't know whether to be comforted by the revelation. She had loved her husband but what was building between her and William was undeniable. What would happen when William found out about her lies?

"Where were you from, Alice?"

Alice met Martha's gaze. This was the first probing question

Martha had asked her. It would be a shame if the first answer she gave was a lie.

"New York, Martha. I was on my way to Wyoming."

Alice held her breath and tried to read Martha's reaction. But Martha didn't react oddly, not even noticeably. She pouted, pulled her knitting closer to her ample bosom and continued her handiwork.

"So, are you still going to go to Wyoming?" she finally asked.

Alice would never complete the journey. She didn't want to go back to New York, either.

"No, ma'am." Alice couldn't meet Martha's gaze anymore.

"It doesn't look like you plan to return to New York."

Alice shook her head. Was this when Martha was finally going to tell her to leave? She had feared this day would come, but every day she'd become more assured it wouldn't. Where was she going to go? And with her rapidly expanding waistline?

"I reckon that you want to stay here."

Alice gave a small gasp. Was Martha going to ask her to stay? That would be an answered prayer.

"Would you mind staying here with us at the orphanage?"

Alice shook her head as a tear fell down each cheek. Martha was beaming widely. She took a freshly knitted scarf and gave it to Alice, who dabbed both cheeks with the woolen material.

"No, I wouldn't mind it at all. I'd love to stay here with you, the children, and William."

"You just have to keep doing what you've been doing, Alice. Help around with the chores. Don't worry about the children. They'll come to adore you. I have a good feeling about you, and I'd be honored if you'd stay."

Alice broke into proper tears while smiling. She dabbed at the salty dribbles and couldn't stop nodding. She wanted to stay.

"I'm getting older, Alice. I need someone I trust who I can hand this home over to when I'm weaker. I need someone humane, with the love of man and the fear of God; someone I can trust to continue in the same vein. Are you that woman?"

Alice loved being at the orphanage. "I-I hope I am. Thank you so much. I want to stay. Thank you, thank you, thank you."

She would have continued her profuse thanks if Tabitha, a small statured four-year-old girl hadn't run into the room. She ran past Martha and into Alice's lap.

"Miss Alice, Sandy wants to bother me with the boo-boo?"

"The boo-boo?" Alice asked, raising her eyes to Martha for

help. Martha shrugged to tell her she couldn't help her with the boo-boo. Alice looked back at the dark-eyed child.

"You tell her to stop bothering you immediately. I don't wanna come in there to get her."

"Yes, I'll go tell her that. Miss Alice will come for her," Tabitha said, with childish assuredness before running out of the room.

"You see, Alice. With time, with time, you'll be their mother."

"You'll be here, too."

"I will. I'll be the grandma." She chuckled.

CHAPTER 9

William heard the sheriff's voice ring again in his ear just before his horse's feet pounded into the many acres compound the orphanage owned.

"She probably has good reason, William. You have the right to be angry but don't blot out reason with anger. You'd probably not do better if you were in her shoes."

Well, he wasn't in her shoes. And he agreed with the sheriff, he did have the right to be angry. And he planned to exercise that right. His stallion moved down the wide brown path that led to the house. It was mid-afternoon, the time the house was usually at its noisiest. Today wasn't any different. William could hear the chattering noise of the children playing in the house from many yards away.

He noticed someone sitting on a rocking chair on the porch.

The black bonnet and wide white apron, told him it was a woman. William assumed, or rather wished it was Alice. He didn't like the way he was feeling and was desperate to get his thoughts out in the air. He rode closer only to see older, more familiar eyes smile at him. It was Martha, busy with her knitting. Christmas was two weeks away. It wasn't unexpected.

"Howdy, William. You're home early. Is something wrong?"

William stopped his horse in front of the porch. He took off his hat, held it in a small hook with the free fingers of the hand gripping the reins and shook his head. He had a good mind to tell Martha all he had found out, to see her become as shocked as he was. But he had visualized asking Alice alone, looking into her eyes as she admitted or tried to lie her way out.

Is she a liar?

He couldn't comfortably say he thought she was. And this new realization made his anger feel misplaced. He liked her and was already making grander schemes that involved both of them. He would have worked his way to them if he had not come upon this new development. But now he felt lied to, betrayed.

She didn't lie to me. I never asked.

But she knew he would never assume this was her situation. What would have been her answer if he asked her to marry him? Would she say yes, knowing she was already bound to another? William's curiosity grew. His anger turned from boiling hot to snowy cold. He decided upon another set of actions.

"William, are you all right?"

William gave a start and raised his head back to Martha. She was standing now, leaning over the railing, and her ears were pricked and alert with worry. He had been lost in thought in front of her. Her precious knitting was crumpled in the curve of her hold on the wooden railing, not nearly so important now that it was obvious something was wrong with William.

William decided not to burden Martha with the discovery of his findings. She was already worried because he looked worried. She had enough problems with the children. He would handle this and tell her everything after he had found out the truth from Alice.

"I'm fine, Martha. I was trying to remember my plans for the morrow."

Martha blinked and visibly relaxed but her brazen eyes told him she didn't believe him. She raised her knitting back to her chest and looked back for her chair. William wanted to ask her where Alice was, but he figured she'd know he was thinking about Alice. Martha had an uncanny ability to read minds. He decided to ask after settling the horse in the stall. He was turning the corner when he heard his name.

"William."

He turned back to look at Martha.

"Are you sure? I'm worried."

William didn't like being a source of worry for Martha. It was one of his greatest dislikes. He hated how she had written countless letters, insisted on visiting, and then had visited him when he had been shot and was recuperating. He had hated the agony on her face when he'd repeated the doctor's words to her. He'd hated the worry lines that slowly crept into her face and became a permanent feature.

At least some of her lines were there because of her constant worry about his reluctance to find a wife, he was sure. Now he had a woman he was immensely attracted to, one that seemed to have dropped into his situation by divine provision. He had even started to think things could work out, until that smirking bounty hunter had showed up.

The last thing he needed was a worried Martha.

He unearthed his brightest, fake smile. "I'm fine, Martha. I have had a long day with the train robbery case, so I just need to rest or spend some time alone."

"I was about to suggest you go meet Alice in the field. She could stand some company."

William smiled, and Martha smiled back. He knew what she was doing. And she knew he knew.

"Are you too tired to go visit with her?"

"I'll just settle Art here in his stall and go meet her in the field," William said.

Martha didn't stop smiling but she rested her back into the chair and continued her knitting. William watched her for a few more seconds before continuing his ride to the stable. He got off Art and led the stallion into the stable. Trying to think of nothing else, he eased the saddle, reins and bridles off his mount and led him into his stall. Then he gathered some straw and placed it there for the animal. He got some water from the drum behind the wooden shack and placed it where the horse could get it, too. Then he slipped out the back, onto the path that cut halfway across the orphanage farms that lay fallow this time of year.

But they had done well the summer before, and William reminded himself to encourage the children to keep up the good work. He couldn't remember being so hardworking with farm work when he was little.

William decided to take the longer wheat farm path than the fence side because he didn't feel like meeting anyone. Despite the cold, he normally came across cowboys or farm hands on the adjacent ranch if he took that path. The long stalks of winter wheat hid his approach and blocked his sight, but William had spent his life on the farm. He knew where he was going.

What was the best way to tackle this? Should he approach

Alice as he normally did then startle her with the discovery? The sheriff told him he did that sometimes. He said the unplanned initial reaction was the easiest path to the truth when dealing with experienced liars. *Experienced liars?* Was she even a liar?

"I didn't even ask her. But why didn't she just say it?"

The question he had asked himself before rose up once again. What would she have said if he had asked her to marry him? Would she tell him yes? An anchor sank in William's chest as he thought about her telling him yes. If she told him yes, then she was nothing like what he thought she was. If she said yes, he'd take her to the sheriff and hand her over completely. A dark shroud enveloped the little cheeriness William had left. He wasn't so sure of anything anymore.

The noise of deep breaths and soft thuds made him look to the left. There she was, in an old brown dress and a heavy cape. She had a long stick in her hand and was clearly enjoying her walk. William felt something stir deep in him. He swallowed a rising clump and watched silently as she moved gracefully through the field. The hem of the dress floundered up and William snuck peeks of her stockinged ankles. He shook his head and decided he had engaged in enough impropriety.

"Hello, Alice."

She dropped her stick to the ground and turned, startled that someone was behind her. When she saw William, she beamed and stood with her arms hanging to her sides. Her smile was full, wrinkling her cheeks and showing most of her teeth. She looked rough, hair tussled in all directions; her cape slightly askew; and her feet were muddy and brown like the earth. But she had never been more impressive to look at. William found the anger he felt at her supposed deceit crawl to the back of his mind. She was delighted to see him, and he liked to be with her.

"William, how long have you been there?"

CHAPTER 10

William walked closer and noticed small flecks of brown on her face. Her lips were dry, but supple, nonetheless. William had to take intentional breaths.

"Long enough to notice you taking your walk."

She chuckled and subconsciously, she pulled her shoulders back and William drew in air. He didn't know what to do with his hands, so he shoved them into his pockets.

"Since you've stayed so long and leisured yourself with watching me, the least you can do is tell me what you want."

"Just moseyed out here to keep you company for a spell." He gazed at the naked apricot tree in front of them. "I'm surprised you didn't climb up that tree to get a better look at the countryside," he teased her.

"I'm not very good with climbing trees, William. And even if I could, I wouldn't now that you're here."

"I'm not good with climbing trees either."

Alice turned to William with wide eyes. He stifled a laugh by covering his mouth and nodded gently.

"I'm telling the truth. I stopped climbing trees at twelve."

"But you did used to climb trees. You just stopped, so you can do it. Please show me how." Now, she was teasing him.

William ran his hand through his hair, and his eyes fell upon the sharp cut of her jaw as she raised her head to look at the tree. Something started to move in him again, so he took his eyes away.

I have to behave myself. What's wrong with me?

"No, you don't understand, Alice. I didn't just stop."

Alice's eyes thinned as she looked at him now. Concern was written all over her face, and William noticed that she now looked very much like Martha.

"I fell and have never gone up a tree since then." He rushed the words, still not past the embarrassment he always felt whenever he had to admit that. Alice took one step, covering the distance that separated them. Her blue eyes held his attention and ceased his breath, and her soft warm palm that dropped on his forearm arrested all thought.

"You're scared of heights? Oh, I didn't know. I'm sorry."

The rush of blood jolted him back. William grimaced and looked back at the tree. He always hated admitting it. Her hand on his arm comforted him though.

"So, neither of us can climb."

William broke away from her hold and picked up her walking stick.

"Look, William! I think there's a bird's nest up there. Wouldn't that look perfect in our Christmas tree? I know the children would love it!"

He stood on tip toe and ran the pole through the air, but it didn't reach the nest. He jumped up and repeated the swipe, but it only almost touched the nest, almost.

"I can't get it."

Alice sulked, gave the nest one last longing look and shrugged. She turned to go then turned back sharply.

"There's a way we can get it, but no one must see us."

Mischief sparkled in the blue of her eyes, and William's interest was piqued.

"Speak on, ma'am."

"If you could, uhm, lift me—"

"No, we can't do that," William said, interrupting her and

shaking his head in vehement refusal. He wanted to do it. He wanted to do it very much. But it wasn't proper and would bring up dangerous thoughts. He turned to walk away but Alice grabbed his hand.

"William. William, wait. I know what it looks like. But" – she placed her hand on his shoulder – "We both know it doesn't matter. Does it?"

It does. I like you very much. And I don't know if I can behave myself. And there's this matter of a bounty hunter looking all over for you.

But William found himself nodding. There was no one around anyway. What was the worst that could happen? She'd fall on him. They'd have a big laugh and go home. Then he'd think of another time to ask her about the past that was catching up to her fast.

"All right," she said, her eyes twinkling. "I'll take the stick, and you just wrap your hands around my waist and lift me up."

William waited for her to return to his front with the stick in her hand. Then he bent and carefully folded his hands around her waist, careful not to allow his arms to ride up. He held her steady and felt her swing above him. He heard a dull thud on the ground.

"Yes! I got it! Now put me down."

She dropped the stick, and he lowered her down. When her

face became level to his face, he paused and gave her the closest look he had ever given her. She stopped smiling and her eyelids fluttered once. William banished his fears and followed his heart. He brought his mouth to hers and kissed her, feeling her lips so soft and sweet beneath his. Her hands were against his arm, and his grip increased with force. William was reminded that he was a man and knew he had to stop this. He broke the kiss hurriedly and placed her on the ground. He took a backward step and waved his hand in front of him.

"I'm sorry. I shouldn't have done that."

Alice smiled. "It's all right, William," she whispered.

William looked at her face again. She was smiling but it was a smile full of worry. This was his chance. He could find out the truth now. He grabbed both of her arms.

"William?"

"Please tell me the truth, Alice. Are you betrothed to Fred Harrington, the Mayor of Sheridan?"

Her eyes screamed alarm. Her mouth opened but she didn't squirm out of his grip. Her gaze dropped to the ground. She didn't speak but that was answer enough. William's hands fell from her arms. Dejection made the cold wind turn frigid.

"So, what are we doing? What are you doing here?"

His voice was pained, broken by the reality of his fears.

William ran his hands through his hair and looked up into the sky. He had been ready to bring down fire and brimstone, but now he only wanted to escape from the truth.

"William, please, you don't understand..."

She touched him on the arm, but William withdrew from her. His breaths were deep and loud, his anger coming to the fore.

"Don't touch me. Don't –" One raised finger broke the sentence. She backed away, and he knew she sensed his emotional state.

"William, I couldn't tell you. I couldn't tell anyone. I can't marry Fred Harrington."

"Why? Why can't you marry him? Why did you choose to stay here when you had a responsibility to get to Wyoming?"

"You don't understand."

"Make me understand."

Her blue eyes were cloudy now, and she opened her mouth to tell him. But William saw fear, caution, and something covering her admission and she withheld it again. Anger bubbled inside him. Why was she hiding things from him? William turned on his heels and started to walk away.

"William, William."

Her voice called him back, and he was reminded of who he

was. He was going to get the truth from her with or without her willingness. He turned and took five brisk strides to her. She saw the resolute set of his eyes and stepped back till she reached the tree trunk. William pushed his hands forward, pinning her to the tree trunk.

"I'm going to ask you a set of questions, Alice, and you're going to provide the answers."

She blinked up at him.

"I'm a US Marshal, Alice, an officer of law. You'd be breaking the law by withholding information from me."

Her eyes still pled, but he didn't budge.

"Why did you travel west, and where exactly were you going?"

"I was going to Wyoming. I was a Mail Order Bride."

"Whose Mail Order Bride?"

Alice raised her hand to touch William, but he grabbed it and pushed it back down. He was angry but he held her hand away because he was protecting himself. His will would crumble if she touched him, he was sure.

"Fred Harrington, the Mayor of Sheridan."

William sighed. He was thinking of building a life with another man's wife. She had betrayed his and Martha's trust.

William didn't know if he could forgive that. But he wasn't done. Some things were not clear.

"So, your trip got cut short by the Haney train heist. You were injured, and we took you into our care. But that was just for a few days. You could still have gone if you wanted to."

"I don't want to, William. Please, I want to stay here."

"Why didn't you just go?"

"On the train, when I was hiding inside the coach where you found me, I heard members of the Haney gang speaking."

William's curiosity spiked. He watched her eyes for any signs that she was creating events, but she seemed sincere.

"Which members? And what did you hear?"

"I don't know. One of them was Henry."

William nodded. Everyone knew Henry Haney, the man after which the gang was named. Henry Haney was the most notorious criminal in the Wild West.

"What did they say that made you decide not to complete your journey?"

"I can't remember the exact words, William."

"You have to remember something, Alice. This is an interrogation."

The wind blew hard and cold. William allowed his eyes to stray behind her to the rough bark of the tree. Her voice brought his attention back.

"Fred Harrington was in league with them. But one of them was suggesting Fred alerted the marshals and town guards. Henry answered that it couldn't be Fred. He was one of them."

William ran his fingers over his chin. Fred Harrington? It all made sense now. William and the sheriff had always wondered how the Haney gang came to know secret locations where huge sums of money or valuables were. Who was their informant? William had asked Marvis. Marvis wasn't close to Henry, so he didn't know.

"You preferred to stay with us than continue to your criminal husband."

"I couldn't go on."

"Yes, I agree with you. But I'll tell you what you could have done—you could have spoken. You could have told me."

William turned and started to walk away. Alice ran up to him and grabbed his hand.

"William, please you can't tell me to go."

"I can't tell you to go. But you lied to me too long, and now a bounty hunter is on your tail. The safest place you can stay is with us at the orphanage. Only a few people know you're here."

William drew his hand away from her grip and started back into the tall brown stalks of wheat, but then he hesitated.

"I'll need to confirm this piece of information you've given me. Find out if it's true." He knew his words would sting her. He wanted them to sting. He was hurt. "Then me and the sheriff can act together to bring the Mayor to justice, but I think it'll take a bit of time to confirm this information. Don't leave the orphanage."

He walked into the field and thought he heard a sob behind him.

CHAPTER 11

Alice normally hummed when hanging washed clothes, especially since she had come to the orphanage. Today was bright. The sun was hoisted high in the sky, but the winter cold didn't allow any heat to reach her. The clothes would dry, nevertheless, even if they froze first.

It was three days to Christmas, and the Christmas spirit seemed to have infected everyone in the house, everyone except William. The children were overactive lately, but Alice found they were starting to listen to her. It would have provided her some sort of satisfaction, but a dark gray cloud cast a shadow over her face, and she wasn't close to chasing it off. Alice wasn't humming.

William is still avoiding me.

Alice had gone back to the house in tears that afternoon after her argument with William. She was grateful to Lacy who had spotted her from the porch and had come to greet her. Concerned, she had gone in to get Martha who rushed out of the house.

"What happened, child?"

"It's William."

Martha had been immediately sympathetic and told her to gather herself. She prepared a hot cup of coffee for her then asked her to tell her what happened. Now, Alice hid nothing from Martha. And though Martha admitted she was disappointed that Alice had been keeping something of such importance from them, she was more understanding.

"You had a past. It could have been anything. I knew that. William is hurt, Alice. You should understand. When William looks at you, what he sees isn't what I see."

Alice almost smiled in the midst of her hurt that evening. That was the closest anyone had come to admitting there was something between her and William. Yes, William had confirmed it by kissing her that afternoon but that happened immediately before he started to drill her. And he was as cold as she had ever seen him be, icily impersonal. He questioned her like she was a criminal, like he had not just taken her breath away with a deep, time-freezing kiss. Alice couldn't count on that kiss now; it meant nothing.

"But I begged him."

"You begged him, true. But you lied to him for weeks. He has the right to remain angry for much longer than one day."

Alice prayed William would not remain angry for very long.

"But I don't think he'll be angry too long. I'll speak to him. Don't panic. And stay here. If he says a bounty hunter is after you, then you are forewarned. Never leave the house."

Alice obeyed Martha. She never went out into the field. The farthest she went was the front of the house and only at night. Martha had spoken to William, but he didn't soften his stance. He left the house in the mornings and came home late at night. He was friendly and playful with the children and Martha, but he was rigid with her. He didn't speak to her and would not meet her gaze. Alice had gone up to meet him more than once, but he brushed away her efforts and gave her cold, one-word replies.

Something ruffled behind her and Alice swung around, hoping it was William, but she saw nothing.

It must be the wind.

Martha had told her the evening before that William had put word out to other lawmen and an investigation was ongoing concerning the implications of her claims. The bounty hunter was still in town, so she was not free as the wind yet.

Alice picked up another cloth and looked at the back door of the house. The children must have been running around inside the house because the noise went up a notch. Alice worried their noise would awaken Martha. Alice hung the blouse and bent to pick a cotton dress when she saw muddied, brown boots behind her.

Those aren't William's.

"Hello, Alice Thompson."

Alice gave a start and dropped the cloth in her hand, allowing it fall to the frozen ground. She turned to see a man behind her. He wasn't as tall as William, and his face was harder and there was a wicked grin on it. His hands were folded into fists, and he stared at her like she was on display, merchandise he was about to purchase.

"Who are you?"

He smiled and took a step forward. Alice automatically took a step back, kicking into the basket behind her, spilling the remaining washing onto the ground.

"Oh, I doubt that you know me, Miss Thompson, but I think you know of me. I'm sent by your husband, dear bride."

"I don't have any husband."

The smirk disappeared, and his frown was almost a grimace. "You know exactly what I'm talking about, woman. It cost me a lot of money to stay in the motel I'm in, hoping for news. It cost me money to bribe people in the town before I found out that our dear US Marshal had a young, unmarried woman hiding in his orphanage. I should have known from his first reaction when I showed him your picture. All that doesn't matter. Christmas is in a couple of days, and the price on you will make my season very interesting, the most interesting in decades."

Alice nervously looked behind her, trying to figure out the best method to get away.

"Don't even think about it."

A small rifle appeared in his hand, and he pointed it at her. She froze.

"If you try to run, I'll have to shoot you. If you die, Fred doesn't pay me at all. If you're injured, he doesn't pay me as much. Either way, I get angry and have to get back at you by going in there to get one of the children, or the matron of the house—the beloved Martha."

Alice shook her head. Her heart beat loudly, banging in her ears. She had never felt so cold.

"Don't do anything to hurt them, please. I'll do whatever you ask."

He smiled.

"Good, because you're about to do a lot for me. There's a wagon waiting for us just on the other side of the fence. You move as I say. I'll tie you up, plug your mouth and take you somewhere. You'll surely be spending Christmas with your husband. Isn't that a wonder?"

Alice gulped. Horrid Christmases were becoming a tradition for her.

Art walked so slowly, William was sure the stallion felt some of his tiredness. The day had been draining, physically and mentally. He never felt fully energized since that day in the field. He had not been able to push away the thought that Alice belonged to another man. She wasn't his, and the reality hurt him bone-deep. William allowed Art to walk down the winding path and take the right turn that led to the small gate in front of the compound. The gate swung in the cold breeze and Art pushed it in with his nose before walking into the compound.

William was as angry with himself as he was with Alice. It wasn't that he didn't want to forgive her, but what was the point? Yes, her claims about Fred Harrington were turning out to be true, but she still had a contract with him. William wasn't going to assume she was free until Fred Harrington was arrested by the sheriff in Sheridan or until he decided he had no arrangement with Alice. And even when she became free, he was a man who had lost the ability to father children. He saw the way she looked at the children in the orphanage. She loved them.

One case of deceit was breaking them apart. Another would keep them apart. William could not imagine asking her to marry him without telling her the truth about his disability. And if he did, if he did...

There was no point thinking about her reaction. She surely wanted to be a mother as much as she wanted to be a wife.

William looked at the porch and saw more activity than normal. All the children were on the porch. Martha and Alice were nowhere to be found.

"Heeyah."

William flapped Art's reins as he called out, forcing the tired stallion into a faster pace. The horse trotted the short distance to the house, and William pulled him to a stop before getting off.

"Lacy, what's wrong?"

Lacy's face was lined with worry. She came down the stairs and disappeared to the back of the house.

"Lacy! Lacy?"

William started around the house, following Lacy when he almost bumped into Martha. Martha was rushing to the front, obviously summoned by Lacy.

"William, oh my dear William."

Martha wrapped her hands around William's arm and pressed her face into his chest. Lacy was standing about a yard behind looking very worried.

"Martha, what's wrong? What is it? What's happened?"

William shook her and set her in front of him, staring into her eyes. She opened her mouth but only wails escaped. William turned around and noticed the other small children were in front of the house. He had yet to see Alice.

"Alice? Where is she?"

Martha wailed even louder and walked away from him toward the clothing line. She bent down and pointed to a fallen basket. Wet clothes were still in it.

"They got her."

William's breath froze. "What? Who? Did you see it happen?"

"Do we need to see her get taken, William? I was sleeping in the house while she was here hanging these clothes. When I came out, I met one garment on the ground. The basket was kicked over and the clothes had spilled out of it, strewn everywhere. We've not seen her since. We were warned, William. We know what happened."

William ran his fingers through his hair. He had advised Alice to stay home, not to go anywhere. Well, she had stayed at home and still got kidnapped. Panic crawled up his throat, but he swallowed it down. He had to control his emotions. Everyone couldn't be breaking down.

"Is there anyone else hurt or missing?"

Martha shook her head and rubbed her face. One of the

younger children came around the side of the house and walked toward them.

"Lacy, gather the rest of the children and get them in the house. Everyone is to be inside the house from now on."

Lacy said nothing. She walked and picked up the waddling, bundled up child, then carried her around the house. William heard her calling on the rest of the children.

"William?" Martha said, pulling William by the arm.

William looked into Martha's motherly brown eyes. He hated to see her so distraught.

Martha went on, "You have to go get her back. I know you're angry about your recent discovery, but I have to make you understand something. Alice would have always had a past. She was running from this past, and we were her protection. You love this woman. Are you going to allow her get taken to that horrible man?"

"Love?" William said, finding it odd that Martha was saying this. He liked Alice very much. Of that, there was no doubt. When he was with her, he was happy. Her smile was like a lamp in a dark cavern. She was beautiful, cheery, and intelligent. She made him forget his inadequacies. She was wonderful with the children, and he always found himself wondering what she would be like as his wife. But was that love?

"What do you feel for her, William? Why do you feel so hurt

that she kept secrets from you? If you let this Harrington character get her, you'll come to rue your decision."

William imagined Alice being handed over by Clarence to the dirty mayor. He shuddered and bit into his lower lip. He would do anything to prevent that from happening.

"And there's something you don't know, Will. She's pregnant."

William almost lost his footing. He scowled and peered at Martha.

"Now, you don't understand," Martha exclaimed. "Alice is pregnant from her late husband. The doctor asked that she avoid stress. Do what you have to and get her and her unborn child away from those criminals."

William took a deep breath and tried to take it all in. Alice was pregnant by her late husband? Something welled inside him. Something incredibly strong for her, something strong enough for him to want to marry her, something he had felt for no other woman. She liked him, too, even though he was sure he had hurt her. He would apologize and hope she accepted him. But first, he needed to get her back. He had to protect her and her child. She was his chance to have a family. Desperation coursed through William.

"Will you go, William?"

"I know who has her. I know where he's been all the while. He's going to try to get on the train to Wyoming early tomorrow morning so she can be with that scoundrel by Christmas Eve. I have to get her tonight."

"Thank God," Martha cried, jumping to wrap her arms around his neck.

"There isn't the time for this, Martha. Only the good Lord knows what Clarence is doing with her now."

CHAPTER 12

Silent Inn was always noisy. It was also the preferred hideout and drinking spot for characters at odds with the law. The owners didn't provide protection to people on the wrong side of the law, but law enforcement typically didn't bother with the inn. It was a tradition in Taos, and it didn't seem to be changing anytime soon.

Is this why he chose Silent Inn?

William had known Clarence was staying at Silent Inn since the first day he had met William and the sheriff. William, knowing the bounty was Alice, had thought it wise to keep an eye on him. It turned out he was right.

He slowed his steed down as he got in front of the building. He had thought about all the possible places Clarence could have taken her, but this seemed like the most likely place.

The workers at the inn knew how to look away from trouble, trouble like a young woman being forced into a room. William's blood boiled as he thought about all the possible situations Alice could be in. If as much as one hair on her head was lost, he would .... William let out a deep breath and rode closer.

He couldn't deny anymore that he loved her. Tumbled thoughts had accompanied him on the long ride here from the orphanage. He would be broken if he couldn't find her, or if she ended up with that dirty mayor. He wanted her and her unborn child. He wanted them to be his family. Could he be a good father? He couldn't tell, but he was ready to work on it. He didn't want her gone. He hadn't enough sense to realize this before now, but it was better late than never.

William got off his horse and walked into the stable where he handed his ride to the stable boy. He walked into the noisy saloon, rapidly scanning all the faces. It was dark already, but there was enough lantern light to see the faces well enough. Clarence wasn't here.

William pulled his hat lower and walked to the counter. A slim young woman was pouring a drink from a barrel into a long-nosed cup. William said nothing as he got to the counter, waiting for her to be done. Once she noticed him, she poured faster and soon filled the cup. She walked to the end of the counter and slammed the cup in front of a customer, causing some of the red liquid to spill over the edges. The customer took the cup without speaking and then, she walked to William.

William had taken out his US Marshal badge and placed it on the counter. Her eyes went down to it and when she raised them up, there was fear in them.

"I need you to cooperate fully with me," William spoke and gestured needlessly with his hands as if asking for a particular service. "Clarence, the bounty hunter is here. He came in about an hour ago with a young woman. Tell me where he took her."

"I don't know nothing about this."

The woman's lips quivered as she spoke. William leaned closer to her, pressing his palm over hers.

"You do. And you'll tell me because I promise you, if Clarence gets away, I'm coming for you. And I'm closing down this establishment."

"You can't do that."

"You want to wager on that?"

She stared intently into William's eyes and soon resignation crawled into her eyes. She looked around for anyone observing them before leaning closer to William.

"He took her through the back. I don't know which room. I ain't lying."

"Is he still there?"

"I don't know. I don't know."

Her voice was starting to rise.

He stepped back. "Tell no one of this."

He looked around again and bounded up the stairs. The staircase was dark, but there was a lamp hanging from the wall at the top. William got to the top and tried to gauge how many rooms were on the floor. Fearing he had little time, he moved from room to room. William knocked on each door till the person inside answered.

There were five rooms on each side, and he had already done eight. Only the last two were left. William took his gun out and held it behind him. He placed his ear on the door and knocked. He heard something, a stifled groaning sound. William reared back and crashed into the door, breaking it open.

He saw her immediately, tied up and sitting with her back against the wall. She struggled harder once she saw him, and William rushed to her side. He took out his knife and cut through the tight ropes that bound her hands and feet. Then he pulled out the rag that was stuffed in her mouth.

"William," she muttered, "thank you, thank you."

William heaved a sigh of relief as she threw herself against him, hugging him tightly. He bent low, dipping his face into her hair and breathing her in. He squeezed her in his arms and then eased her off him. He needed to talk to her. He glanced around and saw that they were alone.

"I'm sorry it took me so long to get here. I was shattered by our argument, but that was nothing compared to the alarm I felt when Martha told me you were gone. I love you, Alice. It took me a good while to realize it, but I love you. I love you and the child in you, and I want both of you."

Alice began to cry. Her face was streaked with dust and sweat, but she was alive and that was all that mattered.

"I love you, too, William. That was why I feared telling you. I didn't know how you'd react. I didn't want you to get angry at me, but ..."

"It's fine now. Everything is all right. We're together now."

William placed his hands on her shoulders and kissed her. Her hands gripped his back as she returned his kiss. William broke the kiss and stared into her eyes. She was the most beautiful woman he knew.

"Where is Clarence?" he asked gruffly.

"He tied me up and went downstairs. He claimed he was going to drink, and I think he was telling the truth."

"Did he touch you?" William asked, his anger brewing again.

"No, he only tied me up. I'm scared, William. He's going to come back."

"Then we have to go before he does."

William kissed her again and was about to stand up when there was a crash on the door behind him.

"You! Wha … what are you doing here?"

It was Clarence and his slurred speech told William he was drunk. He had a rifle in his hand, pointed straight at William, and William didn't doubt he would use it. He started to stand up. Alice tried to hold him down, but he shrugged her off.

"Clarence, we'll deal with this like men."

Clarence chuckled. "Men? That's how we're dealing with this, like men? A gunfight then." Clarence swayed as he spoke, and his eyelids were almost completely shut.

William suspected he didn't have good aim, but he wasn't willing to bet on that. Even without great aim, William was close enough to get shot in the chest. He started to circle the room, getting Clarence's aim away from Alice.

"What do you think you are doing, mister? I'm not here to dance with you. You – You stand between me and my money. I can't let you go."

"There's no money for you, Clarence. I've sent word to Sheridan. The mayor will be in jail by noon tomorrow. You've worked for nothing."

Clarence's eyebrows arched. It was obvious he was

contemplating William's words. Seeing the effect, William continued.

"But if you surrender now, I'll convince the sheriff to let you off. You didn't commit any crime because no one is hurt. Alice isn't hurt."

Clarence's eyes showed uncertainty. He snuck a peek at Alice and then turned to look properly at her. William saw his chance. He leapt across the room as Clarence turned back. William grabbed the gun and tried to wring it free of Clarence's grip.

Alice heard a loud bang, and the two men fell down.

"William!" she shrieked.

Alice ran across to William and slowly rolled him off Clarence. His eyes were closed but his breathing was steady. The gun lay just between their heads and Alice used her foot to kick it away. She looked over William's body and found no injury, no blood. William opened his eyes.

"William," Alice cried before bending low to kiss him. Then she raised her head and smacked him. "Don't ever scare me like that again."

There was a cough, and Clarence's cackling voice. "Help me."

Alice turned to look at Clarence. There was a pool of blood

on his belly, and it was spreading. His breaths were hoarse wheezes.

"He's dying. William, he's dying."

"Go find help."

Alice ran out of the room and down the stairs. The bang of the gunshot must have been heard in the saloon because it was almost empty and even the barkeeps were hiding.

"We need a doctor," Alice shouted.

A head slowly rose above the counter. It was a slim young woman. "Is it the marshal who was shot?"

Alice shook her head. No, thank God, it wasn't William.

"The bounty hunter. He needs help."

The woman walked out from behind the counter. "I can get the doctor."

"Please do so quickly. He's dying."

The woman left, and Alice ran back upstairs.

CHAPTER 13

The evening of Christmas was meant to be cold, but the living room of the orphanage was so filled with excitement that Alice felt no cold at all. She sat and watched as the children ran about in their new socks, mittens, and scarves. Martha and William were speaking and laughing while Lacy appeared from the kitchen with a tray.

"Here we go."

It was steaming hot milk and raisin cookies, a favorite for the children. The children settled down on the chairs, and Lacy walked from one child to another, allowing each to pick two cookies and a cup of milk. The tray was soon empty, and Lacy went back into the kitchen to get the rest. Alice got up and followed, so she could also help.

She was about to step out of the room when she heard William behind her.

"Alice?"

She turned to look at him. Yesterday, she had been overwhelmed with fear when that gun had gone off. When she got to William and found him unhurt, her relief had been incredible. They had stayed with Clarence till the sheriff and the doctor came to get him. He was still alive, and William told her they would interrogate him. All that didn't matter to her. William had told her he loved her. A simple sentence that made her feel all fuzzy and safe inside.

"I want to talk to you," William said now.

He held her hand in front of Martha and the children. He had never done that. Alice couldn't hold back her smile.

"I'm about to go help Lacy."

"Yes, I know. I just wanted to tell you a few things."

Alice looked to the side. They were in the middle of the salon and everyone was staring at them. She turned and saw that Lacy was back and even she was staring. Worry started to creep into her chest.

"Is something wrong, William?"

William shook his head and went down to his knee. Alice gasped and looked at Martha, who was smiling knowingly. Could this be what she thought it was?

"Alice Thompson, I've only known you for weeks, and I wish I had known you all my life. Everything is brighter when I'm with you. Everyone in this home loves you. I love you, too. And yes, we've had problems, but we've overcome them, and we'll overcome any other problems that arise. I want to spend the rest of my life with you, to wake up next to you, to be your confidante, your best friend and your husband. For a while now, I've not seen a future, my future, without you in it. Please, Alice, will you marry me?"

Alice covered her mouth with one palm and could feel the eyes of everyone in the room on her. She had only one answer for William. She loved him as much as he loved her, and she wanted nothing more than to spend the rest of her life with him. She took both of his hands and drew him to his feet.

"Yes, William, yes. I'll marry you."

The children laughed and everyone clapped. Alice kissed William and hugged him tight.

The horseman approached and William hugged Alice tighter. They were sitting on the steps, watching the drowning sun with Alice resting her back on him. Martha sat on the porch above them, covered in a quilt, rocking and knitting.

"Are you expecting anyone?" Alice asked him.

"No," William replied. "But I don't need to. It's the sheriff."

Sheriff Nate rode to a stop in front of William and got off his horse. Pulling it by the reins, he walked closer to them.

"Sheriff, it's been a while since we've seen you," Martha said.

"Martha Parish, it's always a pleasure to see you. Merry Christmas."

"Dear me, forget my bad manners. Merry Christmas, Sheriff, please come in for some warm milk and something to munch on."

Sheriff Nate smiled and shook his head. "I'm sorry, but I'm not going to be here long."

William watched his friend's face. He started to stand up, but the sheriff waved him down.

"Don't bother standing, William. I brought good news."

Alice gripped William's hands.

"Clarence Griffin has agreed to provide information on Fred Harrington in exchange for a more lenient sentence."

Alice squeezed William's hands tighter. William understood her angst. It was a few days after Christmas, and this was a new year present for them. They had spoken about a lot of things in that week and one of her fears was that Fred Harrington would remain free.

"Has he started squealing?" William asked.

"He has. Fred Harrington will be spending a lot of the new year in the county jail. You have no ties to him anymore, Alice."

Alice nodded. "Thank you. Thank you very much, Sheriff."

Sheriff Nate nodded and started to go back.

"You'll be coming to our wedding, right?" she asked.

"Wedding? What wedding?" The sheriff was already on his horse again. He raised his hat and stared at William.

"Alice and I will be getting married soon. I'll let you know the details."

The sheriff smiled and nodded. "You know I won't be missing it."

"You had better not," William replied and watched his friend ride away.

William knew there would be a lot of happiness in his future. Alice kissed his hand, and he felt the truth of his thoughts in her touch.

The End

CONTINUE READING...

Thank you for reading *The Bride's Orphan Christmas!* Are you wondering what to read next? Why not read *Pa's Christmas Wish?* **Here's a peek for you:**

Sophie Watson blew her new husband Henry a kiss and waved goodbye to him as he rode out to mend fences. She watched until he and Dusty, the hired hand, were out of sight, then giggled in excitement. It was time to test her plan. With Henry's parents, Charles and Olivia, gone into town for the day, it was the perfect time to see if she had perfected her Christmas present for Henry.

She hurried up to her room and changed into a split riding skirt and slipped on a pair of boots. Then she hustled out toward the barn where a dozen or more horses stood in the pasture, nibbling at the grass that peeked above the thin layer of snow on the ground. It seemed like there were more horses than usual, and she didn't see the one Dusty had been teaching her on. Well, there was one who looked a lot like Daisy. They were likely not that much different.

Sophie slipped into the barn and gathered up the necessities: saddle, bit, blanket, then headed out into the corral. The white horse was near the fence, so she dropped the saddle on the top row of the fence and moved over to her target.

The horse seemed to fight the bit, but she persisted until it was in place, then plopped the blanket on and reached for the saddle. Darn, she was too short to reach the horse's back. She patted the stallion's neck then led it closer to the fence and climbed up on the next to the top slat.

The horse snorted in warning as she heaved the saddle onto its back. It pranced around skittishly as she fastened the cinch beneath its belly. There. She was now ready for her first solo ride. Henry would be so happy to discover she had learned to ride.

Speaking of Henry, wasn't that him riding back toward the ranch? He must have forgotten something. Now, she hurried to climb into the saddle before he noticed her. She wanted to be astride when he saw her.

She dropped into the saddle and grabbed the reins. The horse shifted as she let her weight settle in, then suddenly the stallion emitted an angry snort and reared in the air, his hooves slashing wildly. She grabbed for his mane, trying desperately to hang on, but it was useless. The last thing she heard as she was thrown off the horse's back was Henry screaming her name.

VISIT HERE To Read More:

http://ticahousepublishing.com/mail-order-brides.html

THANKS FOR READING!

Friends, Don't Miss Any News

If you **love Mail Order Bride Romance, Visit Here**

https://wesrom.subscribemenow.com/

to find out about all **New Susannah Calloway Romance Releases! We will let you know as soon as they become available!**

If you enjoyed *The Bride's Orphan Christmas*, would you kindly take a couple minutes to leave a positive review on Amazon? It only takes a moment, and positive reviews truly make a difference. Thank you so much! I appreciate it!

Turn the page to discover more Mail Order Bride Romances just for you!

ABOUT THE AUTHOR

Susannah has always been intrigued with the Western movement - prairie days, mail-order brides, the gold rush, frontier life! As a writer, she's excited to combine her love of story with her love of all that is Western. Presently, Susannah lives in Wyoming with her hubby and their three amazing children.

www.ticahousepublishing.com
contact@ticahousepublishing.com

f

Made in the USA
Monee, IL
20 February 2025

12589966R10066